JAN BRETT
The 3 Little Dassies

G. P. PUTNAM'S SONS
AN IMPRINT OF PENGUIN GROUP (USA) INC.

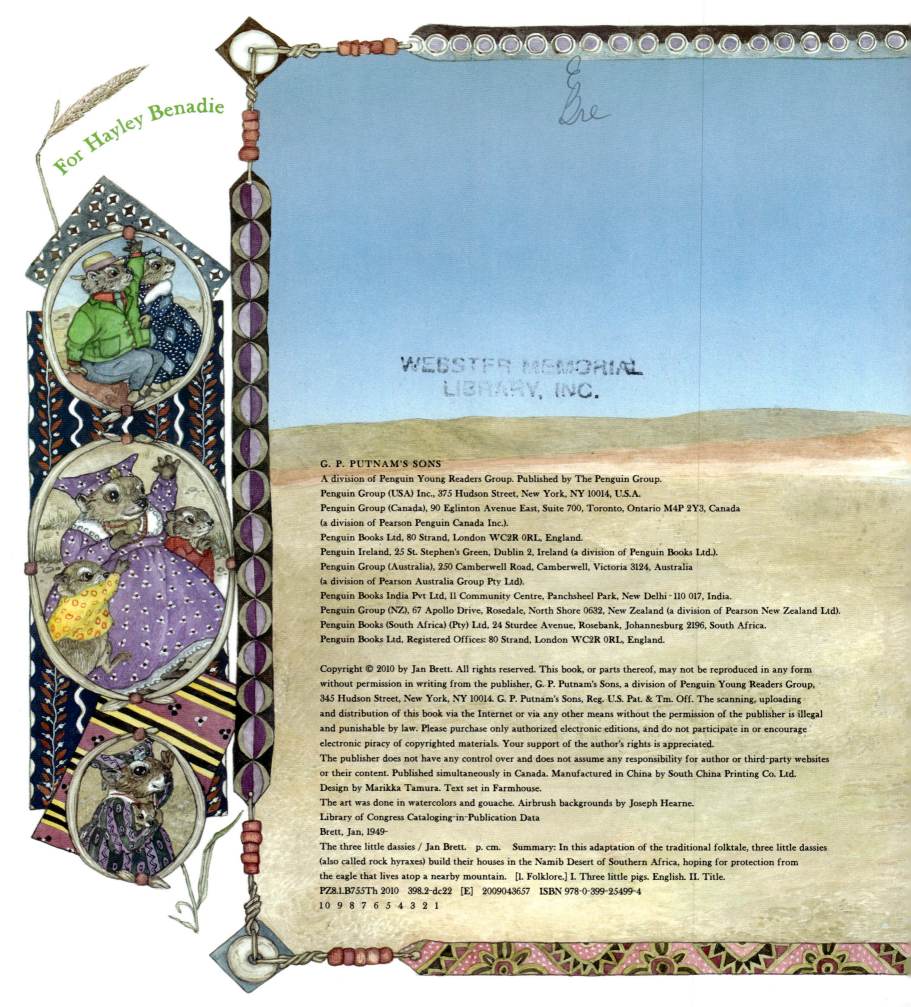

For Hayley Benadie

G. P. PUTNAM'S SONS
A division of Penguin Young Readers Group. Published by The Penguin Group.
Penguin Group (USA) Inc., 375 Hudson Street, New York, NY 10014, U.S.A.
Penguin Group (Canada), 90 Eglinton Avenue East, Suite 700, Toronto, Ontario M4P 2Y3, Canada
(a division of Pearson Penguin Canada Inc.).
Penguin Books Ltd, 80 Strand, London WC2R 0RL, England.
Penguin Ireland, 25 St. Stephen's Green, Dublin 2, Ireland (a division of Penguin Books Ltd.).
Penguin Group (Australia), 250 Camberwell Road, Camberwell, Victoria 3124, Australia
(a division of Pearson Australia Group Pty Ltd).
Penguin Books India Pvt Ltd, 11 Community Centre, Panchsheel Park, New Delhi - 110 017, India.
Penguin Group (NZ), 67 Apollo Drive, Rosedale, North Shore 0632, New Zealand (a division of Pearson New Zealand Ltd).
Penguin Books (South Africa) (Pty) Ltd, 24 Sturdee Avenue, Rosebank, Johannesburg 2196, South Africa.
Penguin Books Ltd, Registered Offices: 80 Strand, London WC2R 0RL, England.

Design by Marikka Tamura. Text set in Farmhouse.
The art was done in watercolors and gouache. Airbrush backgrounds by Joseph Hearne.
Library of Congress Cataloging-in-Publication Data
Brett, Jan, 1949-
The three little dassies / Jan Brett.   p. cm.   Summary: In this adaptation of the traditional folktale, three little dassies
(also called rock hyraxes) build their houses in the Namib Desert of Southern Africa, hoping for protection from
the eagle that lives atop a nearby mountain.   [1. Folklore.] I. Three little pigs. English. II. Title.
PZ8.1.B755Th 2010   398.2-dc22   [E]   2009043657   ISBN 978-0-399-25499-4
10 9 8 7 6 5 4 3 2 1

Hot, hot, hot! The little dassies were almost grown up and it was time for them to find their own place. Mimbi, Pimbi, and Timbi waved good-bye to Mommy, Daddy, aunties, uncles, and all their cousins and set out for the distant mountain.

"Come and visit us!" they shouted. "A place cooler! A place less crowded! A place safe from big eagles!"

The sisters traveled all day and all night across the Namib Desert, arriving at the foot of the mountain the next morning. "This is where we will live," they agreed excitedly.

"Welcome," a squeaky voice called out from the scree. It came from a handsome, smiling Agama Man.

"No one has lived here for a long, long time.
Just me and a family of eagles up on the mountain."
Eagles? The three little dassies shivered
in the hot, hot sun.

Where would they build their houses?

Mimbi eyed the long grasses. "These grasses will make a lovely cool house," she said, and she set to work cutting, twisting, braiding, and bundling. She finished in no time. "Be near and dear, sisters," she said, crawling inside for a nap.

Pimbi spotted pieces of driftwood,
silver from the sun, lying in the sand of the dry
riverbed. "These will make a fine wooden house,"
she said, and she set about collecting as many
pieces as she could find.

When it was finished, she hung up a hammock
and called out, "Be near and dear, sisters, while
I rest my eyes."

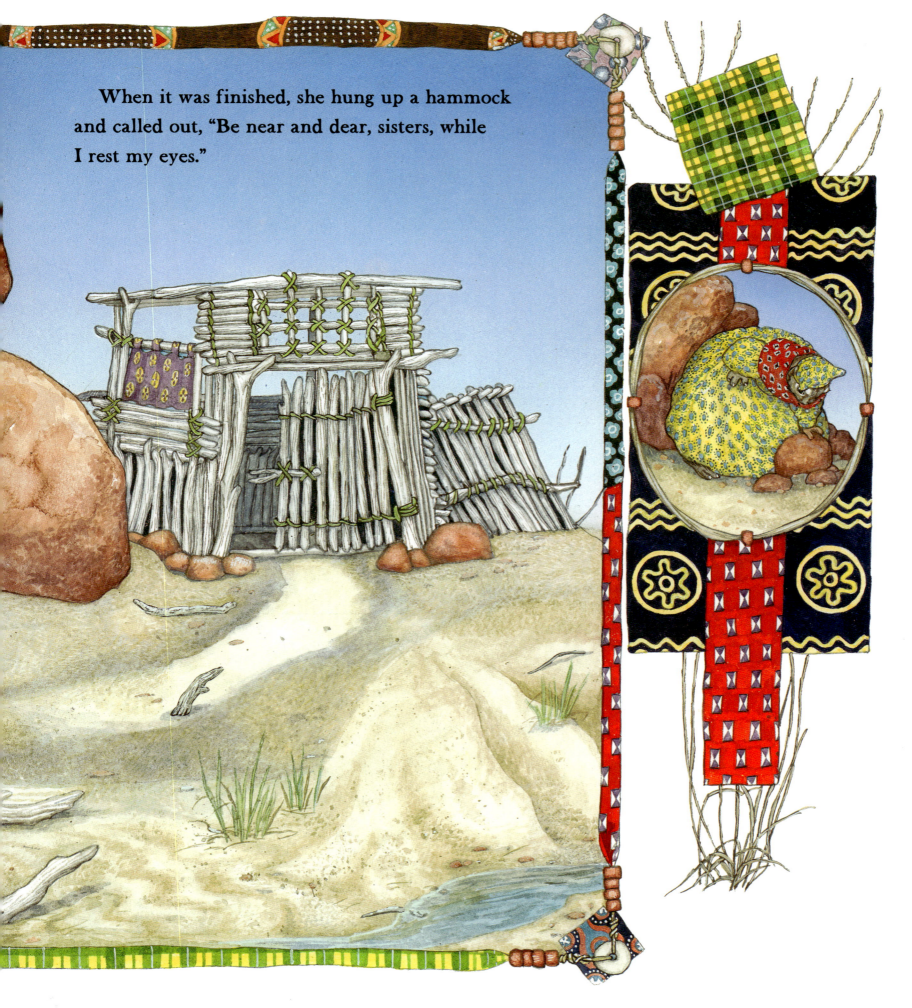

Timbi looked at the rocks around their mountain.
"I will make a stone house," she said, "but it won't be as
easy to build as one made of grasses or sticks."

And it wasn't. She had to work all day in
the hot sun to get it finished in time to sleep in it
that night.

Agama Man had been watching them. He was happy
they were staying on. He had missed having company.

The three little dassies slept late into the morning as the sun rose higher and higher in the sky.

The big old eagle who lived up on the mountain stretched his wings and flew down to look for a meal for his hungry chicks.

Mimbi woke up hungry and went outside.
Suddenly a long-winged shadow passed over her.
"The eagle!" she cried, and hurried back into
her grass house.

"I see you, dassie," the eagle screeched and swooped down. "I'll flap and I'll clap and I'll blow your house in!" he squawked, beating the air with his wings until the grass roof sailed off. The eagle grabbed Mimbi and lifted her up, up, up to his nest.

But the eagle was greedy. No sooner had he dropped Mimbi into the nest than he spotted Pimbi in front of her stick house far below. *Two dassies would be double delicious,* he thought, and down he went, feathers flying.

Pimbi looked up and saw him coming. She turned and ran back inside.

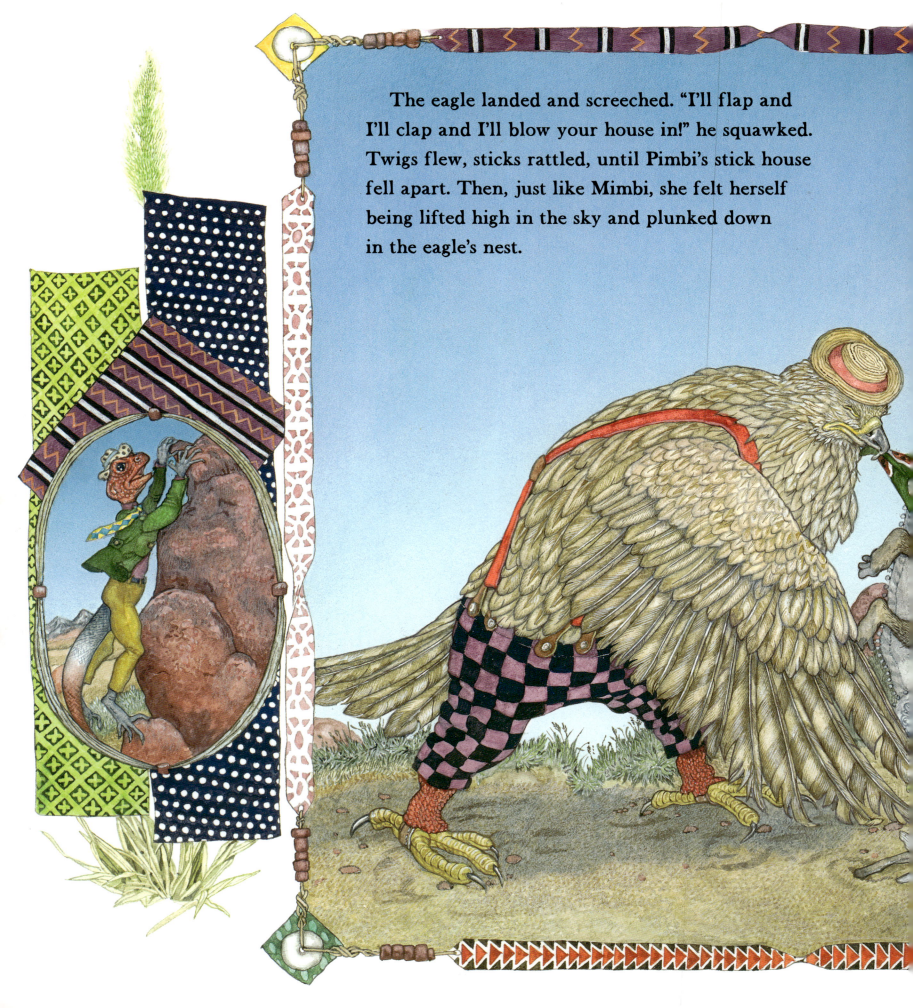

The eagle landed and screeched. "I'll flap and I'll clap and I'll blow your house in!" he squawked. Twigs flew, sticks rattled, until Pimbi's stick house fell apart. Then, just like Mimbi, she felt herself being lifted high in the sky and plunked down in the eagle's nest.

Timbi looked out to call her sisters to come for a breakfast of tasty seed porridge. But instead of a grass house and a stick house, she saw a long shadow streaking across the rocks.

"I see you, dassie! Here I come!"

The eagle landed and shrieked, "I'll flap and I'll clap and I'll blow your house in!" He flapped and clapped and beat his wings.

Dust and sand blew everywhere. But the stone house didn't move. He tried again, flapping and clapping even harder. Dust and sand got in his eyes, but the stone house didn't budge.

When the dust settled, the stone house was still standing, but the eagle was coughing and sneezing. His wing feathers were bent and broken, and he was missing tail feathers. Knowing when to quit, he hopped his way up to his nest. At least he had two dassies waiting for his dinner.

The eagle reached his nest, but the dassies were gone. He looked down and saw them at the bottom of the mountain, heading for the stone house. It was his last chance. He streaked down toward the open chimney.

Inside, the three sisters hugged each other. "There's nothing like a stone house when there are eagles abundant!" they cried.

Just then, the eagle tumbled down the chimney.

"I'll flap and I'll clap and I'll"—*a hot blast from the fire hit him*—"fly home for a nap!" he squealed.

As fast as he could, he squeezed back up the chimney and flew home, all black and singed from the smoky fire. And Mimbi, Pimbi, and Timbi never saw so much as a tail feather of that eagle ever again.

Mommy, Daddy, aunties, uncles, and all their
cousins—and Agama Man too—had come to celebrate.
"Welcome!" the sisters cried. "To a place cooler.
To a place less crowded. To a place safe from eagles!"

And if you travel to Namibia today, you will see dassies living
in stone houses with handsome agama men looking out for them.
As for the pesky eagles, they are easily spotted, for their feathers
are as black as soot.